KING TOWNSHIP PUBLIC LIBRARY

TRISAN

TRI

21.95

32170130779419

I am big

Aug. 23, 2023

S0-BBT-576

Library and Archives Canada Cataloguing in Publication

Title: I am big / written by Itah Sadu ; illustrated by Marley Berot.
Names: Sadu, Itah, 1961- author. | Berot, Marley, illustrator.
Identifiers: Canadiana (print) 20220464871 | Canadiana (ebook) 2022046488X | ISBN
    9781772603125 (hardcover) | ISBN 9781772603347 (softcover) | ISBN 9781772603316
    (Kindle) | ISBN 9781772603132 (EPUB)
Classification: LCC PS8637.A335 I2 2023 | DDC jC813/.6—dc23

Copyright text © 2023 Itah Sadu
Copyright cover and illustrations © 2023 Marley Berot
Edited by Kathryn Cole

Printed and bound in Canada

Second Story Press gratefully acknowledges the support of the Ontario Arts Council and
the Canada Council for the Arts for our publishing program. We acknowledge the financial
support of the Government of Canada through the Canada Book Fund.

ONTARIO ARTS COUNCIL
CONSEIL DES ARTS DE L'ONTARIO
an Ontario government agency
un organisme du gouvernement de l'Ontario

Conseil des Arts
du Canada

Canada Council
for the Arts

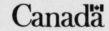

Funded by the Government of Canada
Financé par le gouvernement du Canada

Canada

Published by
Second Story Press
20 Maud Street, Suite 401
Toronto, Ontario, Canada
M5V 2M5
www.secondstorypress.ca

My mother, Gloria Walcott, who at the age of 90 continues to be unstoppable; Don Simpson who cheered on from the sidelines; Nigel Barriffee for the first feedback of encouragement; Ruby and Glen Eversley and their children, Ajamu, Aisha, Jahi, and Kaiso; Zephine Wailoo, Oscar Wailoo, Amani Wailoo, and Shaka Wailoo.

All Black hockey families who show up daily at hockey rinks out of sheer determination to see their Canadian children excel and succeed.

The Perryman family: Abena, Ellis, Ayanna, and Malik. Thank you for your advocacy, your heart, and keeping the spirit of hope and courage alive. Sojo and Miguel, my biggest fans.

To Black boys in hockey, we see your talent and style. We see how beautifully skillful you are.

—I.S.

I AM BIG

Written by Itah Sadu
Illustrated by Marley Berot

Second Story Press

I am nine years old and I am a little kid, but I am **big** in size.

How can you be small and **big** at the same time?

What do you see,
when you see me?

Small and **big**
or **big** and small?

My mother says I am mighty. That's big.

My father says I am strong, and an awesome big feeling comes over me.

Like the feeling of
freedom as I skate and fly
with speed, lining up my
play behind the puck
on my way to the goal.

But, but
big can also be
BAD for a boy.
A big boy.

And dangerous too,
for a big Black boy.

"Coach, remove that bully!"

I skate and I deke,
avoiding the boards
and the hits.

Do you really see me?
Small and big. Big and small.
Big Black boy.

The rink is ice, ice is water, water is oceans,
and oceans are really big!

The ice washes away all the small
thinking in the arena.

And in that moment, I am a little drop of water.

Moving to a ripple,
about to be a wave
when I land the goal.

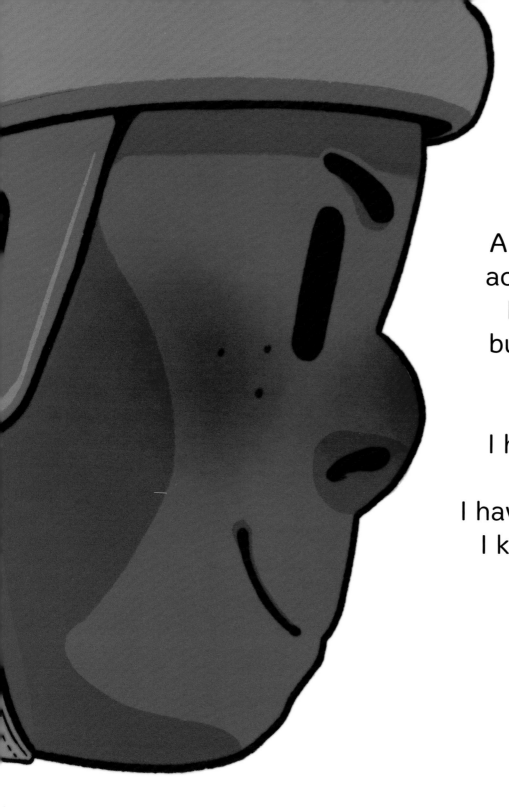

A player skates
across my path.
He is bigger,
but everyone is
quiet.

I have seen him
before.
I have seen his play.
I know his game.

What happens when **big** meets **bigger?** Everyone stays quiet.

Never once taking my
eyes off the target,
I look to the goal.
Time to score.

I skate with grace
straight at the goalie.
His eyes are clear.

He does not see a bully.

He sees big style
and big skill.

He sees ME!

Their voices grow louder.
They fill me up.
I feel unstoppable.
I am in a dance with the goalie,
never once letting my eyes waver.

Like Willie O'Ree
who came before me.

"YOU GOT THIS!"
my sister shouts.

"GO FOR IT!"
screams my brother.
And I sink the puck
into the net.

"SCORE!" my family shouts.
"GOAL!" my team cheers.

The arena erupts and in that moment
I feel truly beautiful.

I AM BIG AND **BLACK!**

Itah Sadu is an award-winning storyteller and children's author. She is the co-owner of the iconic Toronto bookstore A Different Booklist, specializing in African and Caribbean Canadian literature. Itah is the Managing Director of the Blackhurst Cultural Centre—The People's Residence. She is a founding member of the annual Toronto Emancipation Day Underground Freedom Train Ride. Itah lives with her family in Toronto.

Marley Berot is an illustrator with over ten years of combined personal and professional experience. Her portfolio includes cover art for *Neuron*, graphic design work for the Toronto International Film Festival, logo design, and book illustration. She runs her own online store called MarleysApothecary.com. Marley is very passionate about her work as an artist, and this can be seen in every piece she creates. She lives in the Toronto area.